ON THE

PLEASURE

DERIVED FROM

OBJECTS OF TERROR

with

Sir Bertrand, a Fragment

BY

JOHN AIKIN

AND

ANNA LAETITIA BARBAULD

(Illustrated)

Edited and Narrated by Tarah Wheeler

Miscellaneous Pieces in Prose

London, 1773

Anna Laetitia Barbauld (1743-1825)

ON THE PLEASURE DERIVED FROM OBJECTS OF TERROR

That the exercise of our benevolent feelings, as called forth by the view of human afflictions, should be a source of pleasure, cannot appear wonderful to one who considers that relation between the moral and natural system of man, which has connected a degree of satisfaction with every action or emotion productive of the general welfare. The painful sensation immediately arising from a scene of misery, is so much softened and alleviated by the reflex sense of self-approbation attending virtuous sympathy, that we find, on the whole, a very exquisite and refined pleasure remaining, which makes us desirous of again being witnesses to such scenes, instead of flying from them with disgust and horror.

It is obvious how greatly such a provision must conduce to the ends of mutual support and assistance. But the apparent delight with which we dwell upon objects of pure terror, where our moral feelings are not in the least concerned, and no passion seems to be excited but the depressing one of fear, is a paradox of the heart, much more difficult of solution.

The reality of this source of pleasure seems evident from daily observation. The greediness with which the tales of ghosts and goblins, of murders, earthquakes, fires, shipwrecks, and all the most terrible disasters attending human life, are devoured by every ear, must have been generally remarked.

Shipwreck in a Storm

Tragedy, the most favourite work of fiction, has taken a full share of those scenes; "it has supt full with horrors," and has, perhaps, been more indebted to them for public admiration than to its tender and pathetic part. The ghost of Hamlet, Macbeth descending into the witches' cave, and the tent scene in Richard, command as forcibly the attention of our souls as the parting of Jaffier and Belvidera, the fall of Wolsey, or the death of Shore.

The inspiration of terror was by the ancient critics assigned as the peculiar province of tragedy; and the Greek and Roman tragedians have introduced some extraordinary personages for this purpose: not only the shades of the dead, but the furies, and other fabulous inhabitants of the infernal regions. Collins, in his most poetical ode to Fear, has finely enforced this idea.

> *Tho' gentle Pity claim her mingled part,*
> *Yet all the thunders of the scene are thine.*

Hamlet and his Father's Ghost - Delacroix (1843)

The old Gothic romance and the Eastern tale, with their genii, giants, enchantments, and transformations, however a refined critic may censure them as absurd and extravagant, will ever retain a most powerful influence on the mind, and interest the reader, independently of all peculiarity of taste.

Thus the great Milton, who had a strong bias to these wildnesses of the imagination, has, with striking effect, made the stories "of forests and enchantments drear," a favourite subject with his Penseroso; and had undoubtedly their awakening images strong upon his mind when he breaks out,

Call up him that left half-told
The story of Cambuscan bold.

How are we then to account for the pleasure derived from such objects? I have often been led to imagine that there is a deception in these cases; and that the avidity with which we attend is not a proof of our receiving real pleasure. The pain of suspense, and the irresistible desire of satisfying curiosity, when once raised, will account for our eagerness to go quite through an adventure, though we suffer actual pain during the whole course of it. We rather choose to suffer the smart pang of a violent emotion than the uneasy craving of an unsatisfied desire.

The Nightmare - Henry Fuseli (1781)

That this principle, in many instances, may involuntarily carry us through what we dislike, I am convinced from experience. This is the impulse which renders the poorest and most insipid narrative interesting when once we get fairly into it; and I have frequently felt it with regard to our modern novels, which, if lying on my table, and taken up in an idle hour, have led me through the most tedious and disgusting pages, while, like Pistol eating his leek, I have swallowed and execrated to the end.

And it will not only force us through dulness, but through actual torture--through the relation of a Damien's execution, or an inquisitor's act of faith. When children, therefore, listen with pale and mute attention to the frightful stories of apparitions, we are not, perhaps, to imagine that they are in a state of enjoyment, any more than the poor bird which is dropping into the mouth of the rattlesnake; they are chained by the ears, and fascinated by curiosity.

This solution, however, does not satisfy me with respect to the well-wrought scenes of artificial terror which are formed by a sublime and vigorous imagination. Here, though we know before-hand what to expect, we enter into them with eagerness, in quest of a pleasure already experienced.

The Voyages of Sinbad - Edmund Dulac

This is the pleasure constantly attached to the excitement of surprise from new and wonderful objects. A strange and unexpected event awakens the mind, and keeps it on the stretch; and where the agency of invisible beings is introduced, of "forms unseen, and mightier far than we," our imagination, darting forth, explores with rapture the new world which is laid open to its view, and rejoices in the expansion of its powers. Passion and fancy co-operating, elevate the soul to its highest pitch; and the pain of terror is lost in amazement.

Hence, the more wild, fanciful, and extraordinary are the circumstances of a scene of horror, the more pleasure we receive from it; and where they are too near common nature, though violently borne by curiosity through the adventure, we cannot repeat it, or reflect on it, without an over-balance of pain. In the *Arabian Nights* are many most striking examples of the terrible, joined with the marvellous: the story of Aladdin, and the travels of Sinbad, are particularly excellent.

The *Castle of Otranto* is a very spirited modern attempt upon the same plan of mixed terror, adapted to the model of Gothic romance. The best conceived, and the most strongly worked-up scene of mere natural horror that I recollect, is in Smolett's *Ferdinand Count Fathom*; where the hero, entertained in a lone house in a forest, finds a corpse just slaughtered in the room where he is sent to sleep, and the door of which is locked upon him.

It may be amusing for the reader to compare his feelings upon these, and from thence form his opinion of the justness of my theory. The following fragment, in which both these manners are attempted to be in some degree united, is offered to entertain a solitary winter's evening.

FRANKENSTEIN.

"By the glimmer of the half-extinguished
light, I saw the dull, yellow eye of the
creature open; it breathed hard, and a
convulsive motion agitated its limbs.
. . . I rushed out of the room."

Page 43.

London, Published by H. Colburn and R. Bentley, 1831.

Frontispiece to Frankenstein (1831)

12

* * *

SIR BERTRAND, A FRAGMENT

After this adventure, Sir Bertrand turned his steed towards the wolds, hoping to cross these dreary moors before the curfew. But ere he had proceeded half his journey, he was bewildered by the different tracks, and not being able, as far as the eye could reach, to espy any object but the brown heath surrounding him, he was at length quite uncertain which way he should direct his course.

Night overtook him in this situation. It was one of those nights when the moon gives a faint glimmering of light through the thick black clouds of a lowering sky. Now and then she suddenly emerged in full splendor from her veil; and then instantly retired behind it, having just served to give the forlorn Sir Bertrand a wide extended prospect over the desolate waste. Hope and native courage a while urged him to push forwards, but at length the increasing darkness and fatigue of body and mind overcame him; he dreaded moving from the ground he stood on, for fear of unknown pits and bogs, and alighting from his horse in despair, he threw himself on the ground.

He had not long continued in that posture when the sullen toll of a distant bell struck his ears--he started up, and, turning towards the sound, discerned a dim twinkling light. Instantly he seized his horse's bridle, and with cautious steps advanced towards it. After a painful march, he was stopt by a moated ditch surrounding the place from whence the light proceeded; and by a momentary glimpse of moon-light he had a full view of a large antique mansion, with turrets at the corners, and an ample porch in the center. The injuries of time were strongly marked on every thing about it. The roof in various places was fallen in, the battlements were half demolished, and the windows broken and dismantled.

He entered, and instantly the light, which proceeded from a window in one of the turrets, glided along and vanished; at the same moment the moon sunk beneath a black cloud, and the night was darker than ever. All was silent. Sir Bertrand fastened his steed under a shed, and approaching the house, traversed its whole front with light and slow footsteps. All was still as death.

After a short parley with himself, he entered the porch, and seizing a massy iron knocker at the gate, lifted it up, and hesitating, at length struck a loud stroke. The noise resounded through the whole mansion with hollow echoes. All was still again. He repeated the strokes more boldly, and louder--another interval of silence ensued. A third time he knocked, and a third time all was still.

At the same instant, a deep sullen toll sounded from the turret. Sir Bertrand's heart made a fearful stop--He was a while motionless; then terror impelled him to make some hasty steps towards his steed; but shame stopt his flight; and, urged by honour, and a resistless desire of finishing the adventure, he returned to the porch; and, working up his soul to a full steadiness of resolution, he drew forth his sword with one hand, and with the other lifted up the latch of the gate.

The heavy door, creaking upon its hinges, reluctantly yielded to his hand--he applied his shoulder to it, and forced it open--he quitted it, and stept forward--the door instantly shut with a thundering clap. Sir Bertrand's blood was chilled--he turned back to find the door, and it was long ere his trembling hands could seize it--but his utmost strength could not open it again.

After several ineffectual attempts, he looked behind him, and beheld, across a hall, upon a large staircase, a pale bluish flame, which cast a dismal gleam of light around. He again summoned forth his courage, and advanced towards it--It retired. He came to the foot of the stairs, and, after a moment's deliberation, ascended. He went slowly up, the flame retiring before him, till he came to a wide gallery--The flame proceeded along it, and he followed in silent horror, treading lightly, for the echoes of his footsteps startled him.

It led him to the foot of another staircase, and then vanished. At the same instant, another toll sounded from the turret--Sir Bertrand felt it strike upon his heart. He was now in total darkness, and, with his arms extended, began to ascend the second staircase. A dead cold hand met his left hand, and firmly grasped it, drawing him forcibly forwards--he endeavoured to disengage himself, but could not--he made a furious blow with his sword, and instantly a loud shriek pierced his ears, and the dead hand was left powerless in his--He dropt it, and rushed forwards with a desperate valour.

The stairs were narrow and winding, and interrupted by frequent breaches, and loose fragments of stone. The staircase grew narrower and narrower, and at length terminated in a low iron grate. Sir Bertrand pushed it open--it led to an intricate winding passage, just large enough to admit a person upon his hands and knees. A faint glimmering of light served to shew the nature of the place. Sir Bertrand entered--A deep hollow groan resounded from a distance through the vault.

He went forwards, and proceeding beyond the first turning, he discerned the same blue flame which had before conducted him. He followed it. The vault, at length, suddenly opened into a lofty gallery, in the midst of which a figure appeared, completely armed, thrusting forwards the bloody stump of an arm, with a terrible frown and menacing gesture, and brandishing a sword in his hand. Sir Bertrand undauntedly sprung forwards; and, aiming a fierce blow at the figure, it instantly vanished, letting fall a massy iron key.

The flame now rested upon a pair of ample folding doors at the end of the gallery. Sir Bertrand went up to it, and applied the key to a brazen lock. With difficulty he turned the bolt. Instantly the doors flew open, and discovered a large apartment, at the end of which was a coffin rested upon a bier, with a taper burning on each side of it. Along the room, on both sides, were gigantic statues of black marble, attired in the Moorish habit, and holding enormous sabres in their right hands.

Each of them reared his arm, and advanced one leg forwards as the knight entered; at the same moment, the lid of the coffin flew open, and the bell tolled. The flame still glided forwards, and Sir Bertrand resolutely followed, till he arrived within six paces of the coffin.

Suddenly, a lady in a shroud and black veil rose up in it, and stretched out her arms towards him; at the same time, the statues clashed their sabres, and advanced. Sir Bertrand flew to the lady, and clasped her in his arms--she threw up her veil, and kissed his lips; and instantly the whole building shook as with an earthquake, and fell asunder with a horrible crash.

Sir Bertrand was thrown into a sudden trance, and, on recovering, found himself seated on a velvet sofa, in the most magnificent room he had ever seen, lighted with innumerable tapers, in lustres of pure crystal. A sumptuous banquet was set in the middle. The doors opening to soft music, a lady of incomparable beauty, attired with amazing splendor, entered, surrounded by a troop of gay nymphs, more fair than the Graces.

She advanced to the knight, and, falling on her knees, thanked him as her deliverer. The nymphs placed a garland of laurel upon his head, and the lady led him by the hand to the banquet, and sat beside him. The nymphs placed themselves at the table, and a numerous train of servants entering, served up the feast; delicious music playing all the time. Sir Bertrand could not speak for astonishment: he could only return their honours by courteous looks and gestures.

After the banquet was finished, all retired but the lady, who, leading back the knight to the sofa, addressed him in these words:

. . . .

ABOUT THIS EDITION

TITLE

On the Pleasure Derived from Objects of Terror

AUTHORS

John Aikin and Anna Laetitia Barbauld

ORIGINAL PUBLICATION

Miscellaneous Pieces in Prose, London, 1773

THIS EDITION

Edited and Narrated by Tarah Wheeler

AUDIOBOOK

Cedar House Audio

www.ingramcontent.com/pod-product-compliance
Lightning Source LLC
Chambersburg PA
CBHW041033170626
46815CB00005B/301